AFTERNOON SUNSHI

PRICE: 2 BITS

 MISS MUFFET
BESIDE
HERSELF
▶ FULL STORY p. A5

FOR PENNY

Visit us on the Web! www.randomhouse.com/kids

Educators and librarians, for a variety of teaching tools,
visit us at www.randomhouse.com/teachers

Library of Congress Cataloging-in-Publication Data
Cummings, Troy.
The Eensy Weensy Spider freaks out! (big-time!) /
written and illustrated by Troy Cummings. — 1st ed.
  p. cm.
Summary: Frightened after the scary waterspout incident, the Eensy Weensy Spider needs
some encouragement from her friend the ladybug before she will try climbing again.
ISBN 978-0-375-86582-4 (trade) — ISBN 978-0-375-96582-1 (lib. bdg.)
[1. Characters in literature—Fiction. 2. Spiders—Fiction. 3. Self-confidence—Fiction.
4. Humorous stories.] I. Title.
PZ7.C91494Ee 2010
[E]—dc22
2009025071

MANUFACTURED IN MALAYSIA
10 9 8 7 6 5 4 3 2 1
First Edition

The Eensy Weensy Spider
FREAKS OUT!
(BIG-TIME!)

Written and illustrated by
TROY CUMMINGS

Random House
New York

The Eensy Weensy Spider
climbed up the waterspout.

Down came the rain and washed the spider out.

Out came the sun and dried up all the rain . . .

. . . and the Eensy Weensy Spider freaked out,

big-time!

"There's no way I'm climbing back up that gutter!" she said.

"If I had a neck, I could have broken it!"

The next day, her story was all over the Web.

SPIDER ✦ INSIDER

SLIPPERY SPOUT
SPOOKS SPIDER
WORLD-FAMOUS
CLIMBER
CALLS IT QUITS!

"I'm sticking to the ground from now on," she vowed.

Eensy was embarrassed by the story. She spent the next few days holed up in her garden apartment.

Finally, her ladybug friend Polly paid her a visit.

Polly led Eensy to a small potted plant.

"This is a perfect place to start," she said.

Eensy took a deep breath and placed one leg on the base of the pot.

And then another.

And another.

And another.

And another.

And another.

And another.

And another.

Before she knew it, all her legs were on the pot
and she was an inch off the ground.

Eensy realized that the first inch wasn't too hard after all. So she took a few steps and climbed another inch.

And another.

And another. . . .

Suddenly, she was one whole foot off the ground and halfway up the small potted plant.

"Awesome," she said.

She quickly climbed to the top of the plant,
where Polly was waiting.

"I knew you could do it!" said Polly.

The view was quite nice. Eensy
couldn't stop smiling.

"Now," said Polly, "why don't you
climb that fireplug over there?"

Eensy stopped smiling. "Are you crazy? That fireplug is twice
as tall as this potted plant."

"Right," said Polly. "That means you're already halfway there!
Don't give up now!"

"I guess I could give it a shot," Eensy said. And so she did.

That was pretty fun, she thought. *Since I've made it this far,*

maybe I'll go ahead and climb that dog over there. . . .

It took Eensy only a couple of minutes to climb to the top of the dog.

"Wait up," said Polly.

"Can't stop now!" said Eensy. "I'm just warming up!"

Eensy leaped from the dog's snout to a nearby mailbox and was balancing atop the little red flag in no time.

From there, she scurried along a fence and zipped to the top of a two-story house. She was so focused on reaching the roof, she didn't even notice that she had scaled a waterspout.

It took Polly a little while to catch up. "Eensy," she said, out of breath, "I can't fly any higher."

"That's okay," said Eensy. "You should fly away home and rest; I'm just going to see how high I can climb."

Eensy winked at Polly with one of her eyes,

but the other seven were already scoping out

a large wrecking crane across the street.

Polly waved goodbye and watched Eensy make her
way across a telephone line to the crane.

And so the Eensy Weensy Spider went on

to climb things much higher than a waterspout.

From the long arm of the crane . . .

. . . to the roof of a two-star hotel . . .

. . . to the blinking light on a radio tower . . .

. . . and finally, to the very tip-top of a rocket,

which, as luck would have it, was just about to launch.

Eensy held on tight as the rocket blasted off.

The legendary climber was treated

to the best view any bug had ever seen.

THE END.